# PANDAS

Written and edited by Jinny Johnson

Highlights®

Published by Highlights for Children, Inc.
1800 Watermark Drive
Columbus, Ohio 43215-1035
1-800-255-9517

Designed by Millions Design
Created for Highlights for Children by
Two-Can Publishing Ltd.
London, England
Printed in the China

Have your own monthly subscription to
HIGHLIGHTS FOR CHILDREN delivered to your
door. For information please call 800-255-9517
or write HIGHLIGHTS FOR CHILDREN, INC.,
Product Information, P.O. Box 269,
Columbus Ohio 43216-0269

10 9 8 7 6 5 4

**Illustration credits:**
Norma Burgin/John Martin Artists:
p. 1, p. 3, p. 18-19, p. 26-30
David Webb/Linden Artists:
p. 8, p. 10, p. 14-15, p. 16, p. 31

**Photograph credits:**
p. 4-5 WWF/Tim Rautert/Bruce Coleman, p. 6-7 WWF/Tim
Rautert/Bruce Coleman, p. 7 Rex Features, p. 8 WWF/Tim
Rautert/Bruce Coleman, p. 9 John Cancalosi/Bruce Coleman,
p. 10-11 WWF/Dr J Mackinnon, p. 12 Dr J Mackinnon/Bruce
Coleman, p. 13 Jant Sauvanet/Bruce Coleman, p. 16t WWF/Dr J
Mackinnon, p. 16b Rex Features, p. 17 Rex Features, p. 20 Bruce
Coleman, p. 21 Erwin & Peggy Bauer/Bruce Coleman,
p. 22 Norman Myers/Bruce Coleman, p. 23 WWF/Kojo Tanaka/
Bruce Coleman, p. 25tl WWF, p. 25tr WWF/K Schaller, p. 25b
Rex Features

# Contents

| | |
|---|---|
| Looking at pandas | 4 |
| Where pandas live | 6 |
| What pandas eat | 8 |
| Movement and senses | 10 |
| The panda's life | 12 |
| Finding a mate | 14 |
| Baby pandas | 16 |
| Growing up | 18 |
| The red panda | 20 |
| Pandas in captivity | 22 |
| Pandas in danger | 24 |
| Lin-Lin's new home | 26 |
| Panda quiz | 31 |
| Index | 32 |

# Looking at pandas

The panda is one of the rarest animals in the world but also one of the most easily recognizable. Its striking black and white markings, bearlike shape, and habit of sitting up like a human to eat have made it much loved.

In fact, however, the panda is not as cuddly as it looks. It is very strong, with powerful claws and a sharp bite. Its black and white fur is not fluffy but coarse and oily to help keep the panda warm and dry.

Wild pandas live only in China. They were first discovered by Western scientists just over a hundred years ago. The very first captive panda was brought to the West in 1937.

Scientists have long disagreed about which family the panda belongs to. Some said it was a bear, others that it was related to the raccoons. Now, most agree that while the giant panda is closer to the bears, it should be in its own separate family with its relative, the lesser, or red, panda.

Although called "giant", the panda is smaller than most bears. A male is about five feet long and weighs about 245 pounds. Females are slightly smaller and lighter.

▷ A giant panda moves slowly through its forest home. Its thick furry coat protects it from any sharp twigs and thorns as it pushes its way through the undergrowth.

# Where pandas live

Giant pandas live only in the bamboo forests of a few mountainous areas of southwest China. The mist and clouds swirling through these forests make conditions constantly damp, ideal for the moisture-loving bamboo that is the panda's main food.

Once, pandas were more widespread and lived at lower levels. But bamboo forest was chopped down to clear land for farms, and the pandas were forced higher and higher into the mountains. Other creatures in the bamboo forest include golden monkeys, the goatlike takin, small deer called muntjacs, and bamboo rats.

## THE PANDA'S COLORS

● Nobody really knows how it helps the panda to have such bold black and white markings. Since no one knows, it is fun to think about this ancient Chinese folktale.

*"There was once a shepherdess who befriended a young panda. At that time all pandas had only white fur. One day, when the girl was playing with the panda, a leopard attacked it. The girl fought the leopard off and saved the panda's life. But the girl died from her wounds.*

*All the pandas came to her funeral wearing black ashes on their shoulders, arms, and legs as a sign of respect. As they rubbed the tears from their eyes and rested their heads in their paws, they made black patches. When they touched their ears they marked those, too. And ever since, all pandas have had these markings."*

▶ The giant panda's bold black and white markings certainly do not help it hide in the bamboo forest. Some scientists think that the markings may warn other animals to keep away from the panda.

# What pandas eat

Pandas feed on bamboo stems and leaves. Bamboo is a kind of giant grass that grows up to ten feet high and has very hard, thick stems. There are many different kinds.

The panda breaks off a bamboo stem and sits down to eat, holding the stem in its paws. Sometimes it peels off the tough outer layer with its sharp teeth before feeding. The panda's jaws and teeth are very strong so it can chew the tough stems. Its throat has a special lining to protect it from sharp splinters of bamboo.

Although it is such an effort to eat, bamboo is not very nourishing and the panda digests about seventeen percent of the bamboo it eats. So, in order to get enough nourishment the panda needs to eat from thirty-five to seventy-five pounds of bamboo a day.

In spring the panda feeds on young bamboo shoots, which are much more tender. It may eat as many as 650 shoots a day.

Pandas will also eat meat if they get the chance. A panda sometimes catches a small animal such as a vole or a bamboo rat, but it is not a good hunter. It will also feed on the remains of a dead animal.

▶ A panda settles down to feed on the bamboo stems and leaves that make up as much as 99 percent of its diet.

## THE PANDA'S "THUMB"

● The panda has an extra "thumb" on each front paw that helps it grip the bamboo stems. This is not really a thumb at all but part of the wristbone. It is moved by special muscles and can be placed against the first finger.

▲ Bamboo stems are extremely tough. The panda must bite through them to get at the soft pith inside.

# Movement and senses

The panda usually moves slowly. It walks on all fours with its paws turned slightly inward and its head bobbing from side to side. It can break into a faster trot but has little need of speed. A panda does not have to catch its food and it has few enemies. Leopards and wild dogs are the main predators in the bamboo forests but rarely attack the powerful panda, which is well able to defend itself.

Pandas can climb trees quite easily and sometimes like to bask in the sun in a handy tree fork. Young pandas

▽ Pandas usually make their scent marks on the ground. Sometimes, though, a panda stands on its hands and leaves its scent on a tree trunk. Pandas can probably recognize each other from these scent signals. They may return to mark the same trees over and over again so the scent signal builds up.

may climb trees to escape from danger. The panda also swims, holding its head above water and paddling with its legs.

The panda sees well in dim light and often feeds at night. Its daytime vision is thought to be good as well. Like most mammals the panda has an excellent sense of smell. It picks up any strange scents in the air that might warn of danger.

Pandas mark trees or rocks in their home range with a smelly liquid from glands near the tail, sometimes mixed with urine. Females mark more often at breeding time. Males can usually tell whether a female is ready to mate from her scent mark.

▽ Pandas climb well. Their strong, sharp claws help them clamber up tree trunks and grip firmly on to the branches.

# The panda's life

The panda has a home range in which it lives and feeds. This area is usually about 1.5 to 2.5 square miles. Males usually have slightly bigger ranges than females. Pandas live alone but their ranges often overlap. If two pandas do chance to meet as they wander the forest, they go their separate ways again as soon as possible.

Most of a panda's time is spent eating. To get enough nourishment from its bamboo diet, a panda has to feed for fourteen or more hours a day. Day and night it wanders between patches of bamboo, sitting down to chew the leaves and hard stems. Once or twice a day pandas go to a stream or pool to take a drink.

The panda does not have a regular resting place but sleeps for a few hours on the ground or in a hollow tree whenever it feels tired. It sleeps at night or in the day and its thick coat protects it from cold and rain.

▶ The panda usually eats sitting down in order to save precious energy.

▼ Pandas move around very little, except to search for new patches of bamboo.

# Finding a mate

Pandas mate in spring, sometime between the middle of March and the middle of May. At this time a female who is ready to mate becomes restless. She makes more noises than usual and more scent marks in her range. She may call from a high spot so the sound travels and attracts as many male pandas as possible.

Neighboring males hear her calls and find her scent signals. They, too, become noisier and more active than usual. Several may gather near the female panda.

Normally a female will bite or run away from a male that comes too close. But when she is ready to breed she allows him to approach her and they mate. The dominant male in an area usually mates with a female first. Afterwards, he goes away and she may mate with others.

## DELAYED DEVELOPMENT

● After mating, the female's fertilized egg does not always start developing into a baby right away. There may be a delay of between six and sixteen weeks. Scientists do not fully understand the process, but they think development starts at the right time for the baby to be born when the weather is good or food plentiful.

▷ Before mating, a male and female giant panda nuzzle one another and wrestle playfully. Once they have mated, the male goes off and has nothing more to do with the female.

# Baby pandas

Baby pandas are usually born in late summer or early autumn. The mother finds a safe dry place, such as a cave or a hollow tree, in which to give birth. This den must be near a good supply of bamboo so the mother can find enough food for herself without moving far. She may produce two or even three babies but usually only manages to rear one of them.

A newborn panda is completely helpless. It cannot move or see but has a surprisingly loud cry. First, the mother licks her tiny baby clean, then lifts it to her breast to feed on her milk.

A panda mother takes very good care of the baby and never leaves it alone. While the baby is still very tiny she carries it in her mouth if she moves away from her den.

## BABY FACTS

● A newborn panda looks more like a rat than a panda. It is only about six inches long and weighs about three ounces. Its mother is about nine hundred times heavier. The baby's skin is pink, with a little white hair but no black markings.

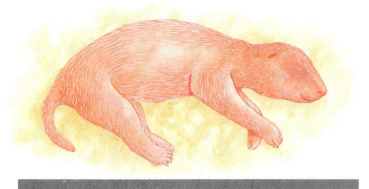

▲ For the first few weeks the mother holds her baby nearly all the time, and lets it feed on her milk ten or twelve times a day.

▲ A panda mother cuddles her four-week-old cub. At this age the cub is still blind and helpless but is trying to make some crawling movements. It does not begin to crawl properly until it is five or six weeks old.

▶ At five or six months old, panda cubs still spend much of their time sleeping.

# Growing up

The panda cub depends on its mother for food until it is about eight months old. By this age it feeds entirely on bamboo. But the cub stays with its mother for another nine months or more. It has much to learn about how to survive by itself. Its mother must teach it how to find food, how to make scent marks, and which animals are safest to avoid.

This is a dangerous time for a young panda, and many die before the age of two. They may be attacked by predators or get lost in the forest.

At last when it is between eighteen months and two years old the young panda goes off to find its own home range. At first, it may only be able to find a less comfortable area than its mother's range – perhaps one on a slope or with less food.

A panda first breeds at about five or six years old and may live as long as twenty-five or thirty years.

## CARRYING A CUB

● A mother panda carries her cub when it is still unable to walk far but too heavy to hold in her mouth. She cradles the cub in one front paw and manages to walk along on her other three legs.

▷ At eight months the panda cub weighs about thirty-three pounds. It is starting to feed on bamboo stems and leaves but also feeds on its mother's milk once or twice a day.

# The red panda

The red panda, with its reddish fur and striped tail, looks very different from the giant panda but is its closest relative. It is also sometimes known as the lesser panda.

The red panda lives in bamboo forest in the same area of China as the giant panda. But it is more widespread and is also found in other parts of China, the Himalayas, and northern Burma. Less is known about the red panda than the giant panda in the wild.

Like the giant panda, the red panda feeds on bamboo, but it also eats fruit, nuts, roots, and small animals and

▲ The red panda looks like a small raccoon. It is about thirty to forty inches long, with a striped tail of up to twenty inches.

insects. It has a smaller version of the giant panda's extra "thumb" to help it grasp bamboo stems.

Much of the red panda's day is spent resting. It is liveliest at dawn and dusk when it does most of its feeding. It lives alone and seeks out other red pandas only in the breeding season, which is usually in early spring.

Red pandas leave scent marks in their territories just like giant pandas, but they also have scent glands in their feet. As they walk they leave a scent trail. These can be tracked by other red pandas or may even help a red panda find its way around.

Late winter or early spring is the usual mating season for red pandas. Litters of one to four cubs are born in June or July. The newborn cubs are about the same size as newborn giant pandas, although the female giant panda is twenty times the weight of the red panda.

The cubs are covered with fur but blind and helpless at birth. For the first three months they stay in the nest hole. By the time they are ready to come out of the nest they are about half the size of the adult. They feed on their mother's milk for four or five months but start to eat other foods at about three months.

▼ Red pandas are better climbers than giant pandas. They spend much of their lives up in the trees, searching for foods such as nuts and fruit. They also sleep in trees.

# Pandas in captivity

Few people have ever seen a giant panda in the wild, but many of us have admired them in zoos. There are about eighty giant pandas in zoos and collections in China, and a dozen or so elsewhere in the world.

Zoo pandas usually have roomy, comfortable cages, with a sleeping area and an outside play area. Most have trees to climb and perhaps a pool to splash in. They must be provided with plenty of fresh bamboo to eat, but they also feed on a range of other foods such as fruit and meat.

Since pandas are so rare, zoos do not want to take too many from the wild. For many years they have been trying to breed pandas in captivity, but it has proved very difficult. The first success was in 1963, when a panda called Ming Ming was born in Beijing Zoo in China. Since then more than thirty cubs born in captivity in China have survived to maturity.

Outside China a number of cubs have been born in captivity. The Madrid Zoo has produced cubs by artificial insemination.

Scientists hope that one day captive-bred giant pandas might be re-introduced into the wild.

▷ To keep healthy, zoo pandas need space to move around and some trees to climb.

▽ Giant pandas are certainly among the most popular of all zoo animals.

# Pandas in danger

Experts believe there are only between five hundred and a thousand pandas left in the wild in China. Most of these are in the twelve special reserves that have been set up for the giant panda. In these, the animals can live in safety while scientists study their behavior and try to learn more about their lives. In the biggest reserve they are also breeding pandas.

It is against the law to kill or harm pandas, but skins are sometimes smuggled out of China. People are rewarded for helping injured pandas or catching poachers.

One of the reasons the panda is so rare is its diet. It has to live where there is plenty of bamboo, and as more and more land has been cleared to make space for crops and homes this has become more difficult.

Also, the bamboo is a very unusual plant. It flowers only once every fifty or one hundred years, and after flowering it dies. All the bamboo of the same kind in an area flowers at the same time, leaving the panda without food. It takes up to ten years for the bamboo to grow large enough to feed a panda population.

In the past when this happened the pandas just moved on and found a different kind of bamboo that had not flowered. But now it is much harder for the pandas to do this. Most are in reserves and there is much less bamboo than there was.

Different types of bamboo are now being planted in reserves, so if one type flowers and dies the pandas can feed on another. Scientists are also considering linking the reserves with "corridors" of land. Then the pandas could move from one to another when necessary.

Many experts are working hard to save the panda, but there is still much more to be done. Even more reserves will be needed where the pandas can live, free from danger and disturbance.

## THE PANDA SYMBOL

● The panda's rarity and popular appeal make it an ideal symbol for the World Wide Fund for Nature. This organization, which works to conserve and help the world's wildlife, first adopted the panda symbol in 1961. Since that time it has been used on all their publicity and products. A WWF team is now working with Chinese scientists on a major study project.

▷ Workers on a panda reserve in China carry a captured animal down to the research center. Here the panda will be examined and studied for a few days and then returned to the forest.

▷ This panda is being weighed by research workers at the reserve.

▽ Some pandas in reserves are fitted with radio collars. Signals from these collars are picked up by an antenna so that the panda can be tracked and its movements studied.

# Lin-Lin's new home

## A day in the life of a giant panda

*Lin-Lin lives in a mountain forest in China. She spends her days wandering about her range, feeding on bamboo. But recently her life has become more and more difficult. All the bamboo in the area has flowered and most has died. Now it is very hard for Lin-Lin to find enough food.*

It was dawn in the forest. Lin-Lin yawned, stretched, and struggled to her feet. A soft drizzle was falling and the trees were shrouded in mist and gray cloud. She shook herself and moved a few steps from the hollow where she had slept.

For a moment Lin-Lin had forgotten the problems of the previous day. Then she remembered. There was no food. The bamboo in her home range had flowered and died and there was little left to eat. Yesterday she had walked and walked and found only a few stems.

She had eaten some berries, but they did little to ease her hunger.

What would she do today? Sadly she padded along on her big furry paws, hoping to find a patch of bamboo still alive. But she knew there was very little hope.

Lin-Lin stopped and sniffed. An unfamiliar scent met her keen nostrils. Strange sounds came to her ears. Something was lurking nearby. She waited, staring in the direction of the noises, which were getting louder.

Suddenly three creatures appeared through the mist. She knew that these animals that walked on two legs and made strange sounds could be dangerous. They were carrying a large wire basket with them.

Lin-Lin faced them with her most aggressive look, hoping to scare them away. But they came nearer. Then a sharp pain pierced her shoulder. Something had hit her. She tried to

keep on her feet but she was very, very sleepy and soon fell to the ground.

The three humans watched, waiting to make sure the panda was fast asleep. They had not come to harm her but to take her to a new home, where there would be plenty of fresh bamboo for her to eat. To do this they had to put Lin-Lin to sleep for a little while with a drugged dart.

When they were quite sure the panda was asleep, the men approached and gently lifted her heavy body. They placed her in the big cage and carried it down the mountainside to a truck.

Lin-Lin knew nothing of her journey. She was driven to another area, carried up a mountainside to a forest where there was plenty of juicy bamboo for her to eat. The men lifted her out of the cage and laid her on the ground. Before they left her they placed a radio collar around her neck. They would be able to track her movements from the signals from the collar and make sure that she was safe.

For the second time that day Lin-Lin woke up. She struggled quickly to her feet, still groggy from the sleeping drug. She looked around her in a panic. Everything was strange. Where was she? What had happened?

Lin-Lin sniffed anxiously at her new surroundings, then sniffed again. She could smell bamboo. She looked up and to her joy spotted a large clump of bamboo stems. She hurried over, broke off a stem, and started to crunch it eagerly. She was very hungry. When Lin-Lin finished the first stem, she picked more, sitting down to eat in comfort. Some of the stems were very thick, and she carefully peeled off the tough outside with her teeth before starting to eat.

Lin-Lin ate and ate until at last she lay back satisfied. What a relief to feel full again. Now she thought she had better explore her new home some more. She wandered off through the trees, sniffing as she went for the scent

marks of other pandas. Spotting a handy log, she paused to rub her bottom against it to leave her own scent mark. Perhaps she could claim this area as her own.

Lin-Lin walked until she was tired but met no other panda. Here and there she saw a clawed tree or smelled a fairly recent scent mark, but there seemed to be enough room here for her. She found a little stream and paused for a welcome drink.

From time to time she made more scent marks. Sometimes she simply rubbed her bottom on the ground, but sometimes she would back up against a tree, stand on her front paws, and rub herself against the bark. She found plenty of bamboo and ate some more, even though she was quite full, to make up for the many hungry days she had suffered.

At last Lin-Lin grew tired. She chose a cozy sheltered spot and lay down with a sigh. It had been a difficult time and a worrying day but she felt her troubles were over. She had a new home and tomorrow morning she would begin to explore more of it and eat even more bamboo.

# Panda Quiz

*If you have read this book carefully, you will be able to pick the right answers to all of these questions.*

**1** Where does the giant panda live?
 (a) Africa
 (b) Japan
 (c) China

**2** Which are the giant panda's closest relatives?
 (a) bears
 (b) red pandas
 (c) raccoons

**3** What do giant pandas eat?
 (a) bamboo
 (b) fruit
 (c) insects

**4** How much does a newborn panda weigh?
 (a) 2.2 pounds
 (b) 3 ounces
 (c) 14 ounces

**5** At what age does a panda cub start to feed on bamboo?
 (a) one year
 (b) six weeks
 (c) eight months

**6** Where do most red pandas live?
 (a) South America
 (b) China
 (c) Australia

**7** How often does bamboo flower?
 (a) every year
 (b) every fifty or one hundred years
 (c) every five years

**8** What does a panda use its extra "thumb" for?
 (a) climbing trees
 (b) grooming itself
 (c) holding its food

**9** What color is a newborn panda?
 (a) pink
 (b) black
 (c) white

**10** How many giant pandas are left in the wild?
 (a) five thousand
 (b) two to five hundred
 (c) five hundred to one thousand

# Index

age   18

baby pandas   16, 17
bamboo   6, 8, 12, 18, 20, 22, 24
Bamboo rat   6, 8
bears   4
birth   16

captive pandas   4, 22
China   4, 6, 20, 22, 24
claws   4, 11
climbing   10, 11, 21, 22
conservation   24
cub   18

delayed development   14
digestion   8
drinking   12

eating   8, 12, 18
enemies   10

food   6, 8, 12, 18, 20, 22
forests   4, 6
fur   4, 20

growth   18

home range   12, 18

jaws   8

markings   4, 6, 7
mating   14
milk   16
monkeys   6
mother   16, 17
movement   10, 11, 12
muntjacs   6

panda symbol   24
paws   8

raccoon   4, 20
radio collar   25
red panda   4, 20, 21
red panda cub   21
reserves   24

scent marking   10, 11, 14, 18, 20, 21
sight   11
size   4
sleeping   12, 21
smell   11
swimming   11

takin   6
teeth   8
throat   8
"thumb"   8, 20

walking   10
World Wide Fund for Nature   24

zoos   22